Hamster Chase

Story by **Anastasia Suen**

Illustrations by **Allan Eitzen**

Based on the characters created by
Ezra Jack Keats

PUFFIN BOOKS

PUFFIN BOOKS
Published by the Penguin Group
Penguin Putnam Books for Young Readers, 345 Hudson Street, New York, New York 10014, U.S.A.
Penguin Books Ltd, 80 Strand, London WC2R ORL, England
Penguin Books Australia Ltd, Ringwood, Victoria, Australia
Penguin Books Canada Ltd, 10 Alcorn Avenue, Toronto, Ontario, Canada M4V 3B2
Penguin Books (N.Z.) Ltd, 182-190 Wairau Road, Auckland 10, New Zealand

Penguin Books Ltd, Registered Offices: Harmondsworth, Middlesex, England

First published in the United States of America by Viking,
a division of Penguin Putnam Books for Young Readers, 2001
Published by Puffin Books, a division of Penguin Putnam Books for Young Readers, 2002

1 3 5 7 9 10 8 6 4 2

Text by Anastasia Suen
Illustrations by Allan Eitzen

THE LIBRARY OF CONGRESS HAS CATALOGED THE VIKING EDITION AS FOLLOWS:
Suen, Anastasia.
Hamster chase / by Anastasia Suen ; illustrated by Allan Eitzen ;
based on characters of Ezra Jack Keats.
p. cm.
Summary: The class hamster gets loose and it's up to Peter, Amy,
and Archie to find him and lure him back to his cage.
ISBN 0-670-88942-3
[1. Hamsters—Fiction. 2. Schools—Fiction.] 1. Eitzen, Allan, ill. II. Keats, Ezra Jack. III. Title.
PZ7.S94343 Ham 2001 [E]—dc21 00-009703

Puffin Easy-to-Read ISBN 0-14-230134-5
Puffin® and Easy-to-Read® are registered trademarks of Penguin Putnam Inc.

Printed in Hong Kong

Reading Level 1.8

Hamster Chase

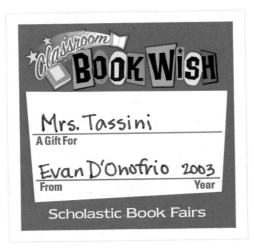

Peter took the hamster
out of his cage.
"I'm going to miss you
next week, Mikey," he said.
"Why?" asked Archie.
"It will be Amy's turn
to take care of him," said Peter.

"Peter," said Amy. "I'm . . . ACHOO!"

Mikey jumped out of Peter's hand.

"Mikey!" said Peter. "Come back!"

Mikey ran toward the classroom door.

Peter, Archie, and Amy ran after him.

"Quick!" said Peter, "close the door."

Archie ran past Mikey and . . .

SLAM! . . . closed the door.

Mikey made a left turn

and ran under the computer tables.

"Not the computers," said Peter.

"He'll chew on the wires,"

said Archie.

"Let's pull out the chairs,"

said Amy.

Peter, Archie, and Amy

pulled out the chairs.

"ACHOO!" said Amy.

"There he goes," said Archie.

"Behind the shelf."

"The shelf is too heavy to move,"
said Peter.

"What can we do?" asked Archie.

"What if we make a noise?" said Peter.

"We can tap on the shelf," said Amy.

"Okay," said Archie.

Peter, Archie, and Amy tapped on the shelf.

Tap-tap-tap, tap-tap-tap.

"Come out, little guy," said Peter.

"Don't chew on any wires," said Archie.

Tap-tap-tap, tap-tap-tap.

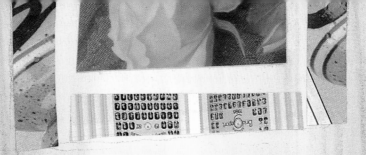

"ACHOO!" said Amy.

Mikey ran out.

"There he goes!" said Archie.

"Follow that hamster," said Peter.

"He went into the coat closet,"

said Archie.

"My lunch is in there!" said Amy.

"Lunch," said Peter.

"That gives me an idea."

"What?" asked Archie.

"Mikey loves to eat," said Peter.

"I don't want him to eat

 my lunch," said Amy.

"We can make a trail," said Peter.

"A trail of food?" asked Archie.

"Yes," said Peter,

"We can make a trail of food

back to Mikey's cage."

"It might work," said Archie.

Peter, Archie, and Amy

went back to Mikey's cage.

"Start with the sunflower seeds,"

said Peter.

"He likes those the best."

One, two, three . . .

Peter put sunflower seeds

in a line on the floor.

Mikey's nose popped out
of the coat closet.

"It's working!" said Amy.

"Don't sneeze," said Peter.

"How will we get him

back into the cage?" asked Archie.

"We can make stairs

with these books," said Peter.

"Don't make any noise."

Archie, Peter, and Amy

stacked up the books.

One book, two books, three books,

four books, five books, six!

"Hamster stairs!" said Amy.

"Put a few sunflower seeds

on the books, too," said Peter.

Archie and Amy made a trail

of hamster food on the books.

Nibble-nibble, nibble-nibble.

Mikey ate his way out of the closet.

"It's working," said Archie.

Nibble-nibble, nibble-nibble.

Mikey ate his way up to the first book.

"Go up the stairs, little guy,"

said Peter.

Nibble-nibble, nibble-nibble.

"ACHOO!" said Amy.

Mikey jumped into his cage.

Peter closed the door.

"You did it!" said Archie.

"Mikey's fur makes me sneeze,"
said Amy. "Peter, will you
take care of Mikey for me next week?"
"You have a deal," said Peter.